Charlie has Asthma

A DOCTOR SPOT CASE BOOK

For Megan

First published in the UK in 2002 by
Red Kite Books, an imprint of Haldane Mason Ltd
59 Chepstow Road, London W2 5BP
e-mail: haldane.mason@dial.pipex.com

ISBN 1-902463-68-4

A HALDANE MASON BOOK

Colour reproduction by CK Digital Ltd, UK

Printed in the UAE

Please note:
The information presented in this book is intended as a support to
professional advice and care. It is not a substitute for medical diagnosis or
treatment. Always notify and consult your doctor if your child is ill.

"The Patients Association recognize the need for literature on children's
health that is educational and enjoyable for both the child and parent.
We welcome the publication of this Dr Spot Case Book."

Charlie has Asthma

Jenny Leigh

Illustrated by Woody Fox

ReD KiTE

Miss Flamingo was doing fruit sums. "What is five mangoes take away three mangoes?" she asked.

Charlie closed his eyes and wished that the school bell would ring. He wasn't very good at maths!

Brrring! The bell rang – thank goodness! The next class was PE, and that was Charlie's favourite.

During PE, Mr Antelope organized a relay race. He chose three teams and made sure he mixed the slow animals with the fast ones. Charlie's best friend Franklin the Frog was on his team, with Mike the Monkey and Geoffrey the Giraffe.

Charlie really wanted his team to win the race, but he was worried because running made him breathless, even more than his team-mates. To make things worse, just worrying about it made him breathless too!

9

Mr Antelope blew his whistle and the first runners lined up.

"On your marks . . . get set . . . GO!" he shouted.

Mike scampered off around the track and was ahead of all the others when he reached the line. He tapped Geoffrey, who set off at a cracking pace.

"Come on, Geoffrey!" yelled Mike, Charlie and Franklin.

Franklin was so excited that he almost forgot that he was going next! He hop, hop, hopped around the track, but he couldn't keep up with the other teams. It all depended on Charlie – he was so nervous!

"GO, Charlie!" his team shouted, and he raced away. Lawrence the Lion was in front, but Charlie just couldn't catch him and Lawrence crossed the winning line first.

"Never mind, Charlie," said Franklin and Geoffrey kindly. "We were too far behind for you to catch up."

Mike wasn't quite so nice. "Huh!" he said. "I could have done it!"

Mr Antelope came over to see Charlie, who was lying on the grass.

"Are you all right, Charlie?" he asked, anxiously.

Charlie couldn't stop coughing and his chest felt tight, as if he had a rubber band around it. Mr Antelope made him sit up and stayed with him until he felt better.

"Cheetahs are meant to be the fastest animals in the world," wailed Charlie. "How could I have lost the race?"

"There might be a reason why you're always short of puff," said Mr Antelope, kindly. "Maybe you should talk to Doctor Spot."

The next day, Mrs Cheetah took Charlie to see Doctor Spot. "I'm so worried about Charlie," she said. "He gets very short of breath and sometimes his chest hurts."

Dr Spot listened to Charlie's chest through his stethoscope. "Do you cough at night, Charlie?" he asked.

"All the time," he replied. "I keep everyone awake!"

"I have a good idea what the problem is," said Doctor Spot. "I think that you have asthma."

"What's asthma?" asked Charlie.

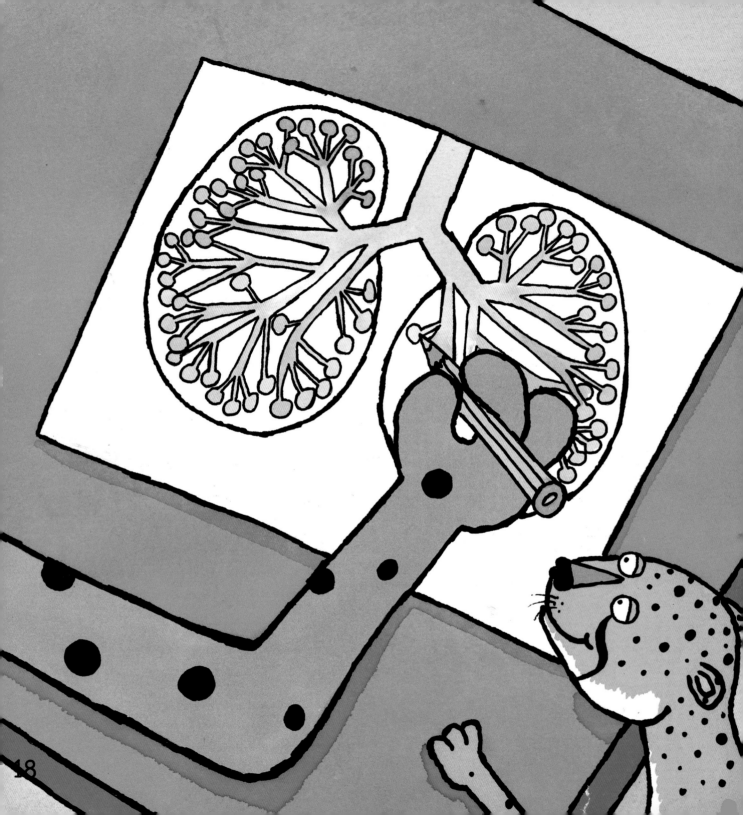

"Well, your lungs have lots of tiny tubes that let air in and out of your body." Doctor Spot drew a picture of Charlie's lungs as he spoke. "If you have asthma, the airways are swollen and tight which makes it hard for you to breathe."

"How did I catch asthma?" asked Charlie.

"You don't catch it like measles," said Doctor Spot. "No one really knows what causes asthma, but lots of people have it. It can be set off by many different things, such as colds, exercise, pets, cigarette smoke, dust and pollen, and often people in the same family have similar reactions."

Charlie looked crossly at Mrs Cheetah, who always sneezed when she cut the grass.

"Can you make me better?" asked Charlie.

"I can't cure your asthma," replied Doctor Spot, "but there are lots of things we can do to make you feel better."

Doctor Spot gave Charlie two inhaler medicines. He called them puffers. The brown one was to help Charlie's swollen airways. He had to take it every morning and night.

The blue one was to use when he was coughing or had a tight chest. It made his airways open wider so it was easier to breathe.

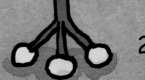

Charlie had to learn how to use a spacer to help him take his puffer. The spacer was a big plastic container with a hole at each end.

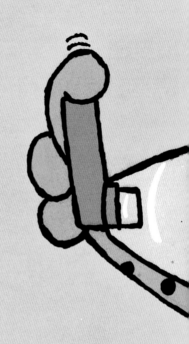

Charlie pressed his puffer into one end and the spray went inside the spacer. Then he breathed it in through the mouth piece at the other end. It was a bit tricky at first, but he soon got the hang of it.

"Can I have a go?" asked Franklin.

"No you can't – you don't have asthma," said Charlie.

Two weeks later, Mrs Cheetah took Charlie back to see Doctor Spot.

"Charlie seems much better," she reported. "Can he go to sports day at his school next week?"

"No problem, Charlie!" said Doctor Spot. "Just make sure you take a couple of puffs of your blue inhaler and do some warm-up exercises before you start."

"Great!" said Charlie. "I'm going to beat Lawrence in the sprint race!"

"Try not to get too excited," warned Doctor Spot. "That can make your asthma worse as well."

Sports day was hot and sunny and lots of animals came to watch.

Franklin was in the egg and spoon race. He hop, hop, hopped – and his egg popped right off the spoon: *Splat!*

"Oh dear!" said Miss Flamingo. "I said we should have hard boiled the eggs!"

Harriet and Humphrey the hippos ran in the three-legged race. Nobody dared to get in their way in case they got squashed and ended up like Franklin's egg!

Charlie used his blue puffer and did some short sprints, ready for the big race.

"Line up for the last race!" called Mr Antelope. Charlie took a deep breath and waited for the whistle. Whheee! They were off.

"Come on, son!" yelled Mr Cheetah. Mrs Cheetah jumped up and down to get a better view. Charlie ran for all he was worth. He streaked across the winning line first, well ahead of Lawrence!

"Well done, Charlie," said Mr Antelope as he hung a medal around his neck. Charlie was so proud of his prize that he was still wearing it when he went to bed that night.

Parents' pages: Asthma

What are the symptoms?

- Persistent coughing, especially at night or after a cold
- Wheezing
- Shortness of breath
- Tightness in the chest
- Any of the above symptoms after exercise or other triggers

What should I do?

- Take your child to see your doctor

Will my doctor prescribe a medicine?

You doctor may prescribe one or more of the following:

- A 'reliever' medicine which can be taken as soon as asthma symptoms occur
- A 'preventer' medicine which, if taken regularly, reduces the chance of asthma symptoms occurring
- A short course of steroid tablets may sometimes be prescribed following a severe asthma attack

What do I do if my child has an asthma attack?

If your child has an asthma attack:

- Keep calm
- Administer reliever medicine straight away, using a spacer if possible
- Sit your child up
- Reassure your child and tell him or her to breathe slowly

If your child does not respond to the reliever medicine in 5–10 minutes, becomes very distressed or unable to talk:

- Call your doctor or an ambulance immediately
- Keep your child sitting upright – lying down will worsen the symptoms
- Continue to administer reliever every few minutes until help arrives

Will my child grow out of asthma?

- It is impossible to say. Some children grow up into asthma-free adults, and some find their symptoms become less severe. Sometimes their asthma improves during their teens, only to recur in adulthood

Doctor Spot says:

- Visit your doctor or practice nurse regularly to ensure your child's asthma is properly controlled
- Ask your doctor for a written personal asthma plan for your child
- Try to identify the things that trigger your child's asthma symptoms, such as colds and viral infections, exercise, pets, dust, excitement, anxiety, cigarette smoke, pollen, mould, cold air
- Inform your child's school about the asthma and ensure that your child has immediate access to his or her reliever while at school. Ask the school what their asthma policy is
- If you are worried or concerned about your child's asthma, call the National Asthma Campaign helpline on 0845 7 01 02 03. Further information about asthma is available on www.asthma.org.uk

Other titles in the series:

Mike has Chicken-pox
ISBN: 1-902463-38-2

Mike the Monkey is all spotty, and everyone knows that monkeys don't have spots! His friends think it's funny but Mike finds it very itchy. Doctor Spot gives him some lotion to put on his spots. Mike has to stay at home for a while, but soon the spots clear up and the itching goes away.

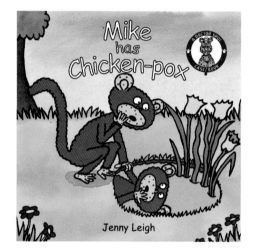

Harriet has Tonsillitis
ISBN: 1-902463-37-4

Poor Harriet the Hippopotamus has tonsillitis! Her head feels hot, her legs are all wobbly, her throat is very sore, and as for her tonsils, they are enormous! Luckily, Doctor Spot is able to help. He knows all about tonsillitis and Harriet soon feels much better.